IGGY BIGGY BUGGY™
One Sunny Day

Written and Illustrated
by Stayci J. Mallozzi

IGGY BIGGY BUGGY™: ONE SUNNY DAY

Visit www.iggybiggybuggy.com

ISBN: 1452844259
ISBN 13: 9781452844251

Library of Congress Control Number : 2010906335
Printed in the United States of America

For my children, Anthony and Stephanie, who inspire me to write. A special thanks to Anthony for coming up to me in our back-yard, One Sunny Day, and saying, "Iggy Biggy Buggy.™"

This book would not have been possible without him!

Iggy Biggy Buggy
woke up one sunny day.

Didn't want to go to school
So he stayed home to play.

Iggy rode his new blue bike.

He wrote his name in the sand.

He played on his swing set.

He blew bubbles in his hand.

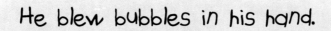

Iggy swung his red jump rope.

He rode his big yellow truck.

He bounced on his trampoline.

He played with his charm that gave him good luck.

Iggy took out his sidewalk chalk.
He drew a dinosaur and a sun.

10

He illustrated some more
Then his creative pictures were done.

Iggy laid down on the grass
And looked up at the passing clouds.

He saw fun cloud shapes in the sky
And then didn't hear a sound.

Iggy started to feel something strange.
He knew something was missing.
He didn't know what that something was
So he sat down to listen.

14

Iggy listened really hard,
Then he realized and found

The something missing was someone.
There was no one around.

Iggy ran quickly to his phone
To call a friend to swim in his pool.

Then he remembered
All his friends were in school.

Iggy walked slowly in his backyard.
He looked at his toys.
There was no one he could share them with.
There wasn't any noise.

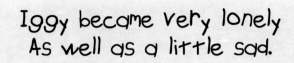

Iggy became very lonely
As well as a little sad.

He missed all of his friends
And writing with his pencil in his purple pad.

Iggy liked to count
All the way to four.

He wanted to learn how to read.
He wanted to know more.

Iggy Biggy Buggy
knew what he must do.
Iggy Biggy Buggy
wanted and went straight to school!

Made in the USA
Middletown, DE
18 September 2022

10724060R00020